The Adventures of Cray on the Bay

CRAY SAVES the DAY

Written by G Pa Rhymes &
Illustrated by Erica Leigh

Illustrations by Erica Leigh: www.EricaLeighArt.com
Edited by Erica Leigh

First softcover edition; November 2020
ISBN   978-1-7348031-5-0
G Pa Rhymes Publishing
GPaRhymes.com

Here's to my inner circle
Four generations of hope and love
To me it's about family
My heart, my soul, my glove
I see the future in your eyes
I see myself in you
A window to the future
My blood, my heart, my glue
This is for my family
Tree top and all the branches
Roots are strong and grounded
We're not taking any chances

I thank you all for the love, encouragement and
constant support.

For my father, Al Wakstein, a history professor at
Boston College, who left this world way too
soon at age 47. He would be proud!

One busy day out on the bay
cars filled the parking lot.
Crowds of humans visiting
their favorite go-to spot.

They brought their beach umbrellas,
some blankets and some chairs,
shovels, pails and kites with tails
for flying in the air.

Giant coolers filled with drinks
and ice to beat the heat,
plastic cups and paper plates,
and yummy food to eat.

When lunch was through
the trash was piled high and overflowing.

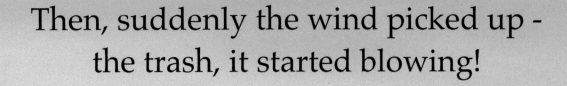

Then, suddenly the wind picked up -
the trash, it started blowing!

Cray the crab watched, helpless,
as the litter tumbled by.
He tried to warn the humans,
but they couldn't hear his cry.

He crawled along the beach
until he ran into his friends.
The fox named Hay and Turtle Fay
were just around the bend.

Fay was in some trouble -
something wrapped around her jaw.
Hay was looking worried
as she helped her with her paw.

Cray rushed in to help them
as Hay's paw began to slip.
He cut right through the plastic
with a speedy snip-snip-snip!

Gull Ray flew down to join them,
saying, "Lots of trash out there."

Cray said, "We need to save the beach.
This really isn't fair!"

"Let's find our mighty mermaid friend
who goes by Queen Mer May.
She can help us make a plan
to clean our home, the bay!"

They found May reading a G Pa book
while sunning on a rock.
Cray asked her, "Have you seen the beach,
the dunes and parking lot?"

May said she saw a lot of trash
from humans on the land
and seemed so glad to see them,
hoping they would lend a hand.

She said to Hay, "You clean the dunes,
and Cray, you clean the beach.
Stand on Turtle Fay
to help you get a better reach..."

"Ray, you've got a birds-eye view
to find the trash that's floating,
then Fay can swim to grab it,
but stay clear of humans boating."

They gathered up the trash until
it almost touched the sky.

The pile got so tall,
that it was nearly 10 feet high!

Farmer Jay came by to gather
seaweed in her truck.
Queen Mer May said, "Hey, my friends,
I think that we're in luck!"

When Jay pulled up and saw the trash she grabbed her garden hoe.

"I ought to take this to the dump,
where it's supposed to go!"

As the truck was leaving,
Cray said without a pause,
"Someday we'll teach the humans
all about our noble cause!"

Kids Learn From You!

Here are some easy ways to teach the children in your life how to take care of the environment!

Think Ahead: Before you leave for the day, consider bringing reusable bags, containers and utensils, rather than single-use plastic. These more sustainable options are a proactive way to reduce waste.

No Litterbugging: What if we left the place cleaner than we found it? When visiting the beach, park or forest, don't leave anything behind. This includes food, toys, containers, paper or clothing. Consider going on a quick scavenger hunt for 3 pieces of trash as a fun game before heading home!

Check the Label: When shopping for sunscreen, look for the kind that's not harmful to sea creatures, coral reefs and even dogs.

Protect Wildlife: Starfish are pretty, but they are alive and shouldn't be played with or taken out of water. If you see seals let them be. Never feed seagulls and other birds. We are sharing the space with them so we need to be respectful.

Stay on the Path: Climbing and sliding on the sand dunes may be fun but it helps the wind and surf erode the coastline. Walk on boardwalks and designated areas.

See Something Say Something: Good stewardship is about awareness. If you see trash, kids climbing on the dunes, or people feeding the animals, nicely explain to them why it's harmful so it can be a teachable moment for all!

"Remember, there are many ways to be an ocean steward, so choose the way that means the most to you. What matters is that you take the first step. You'll be amazed at the ripple effect it can have!"

- Sara Sperber; Operations and Programs Coordinator; **National Marine Life Center**